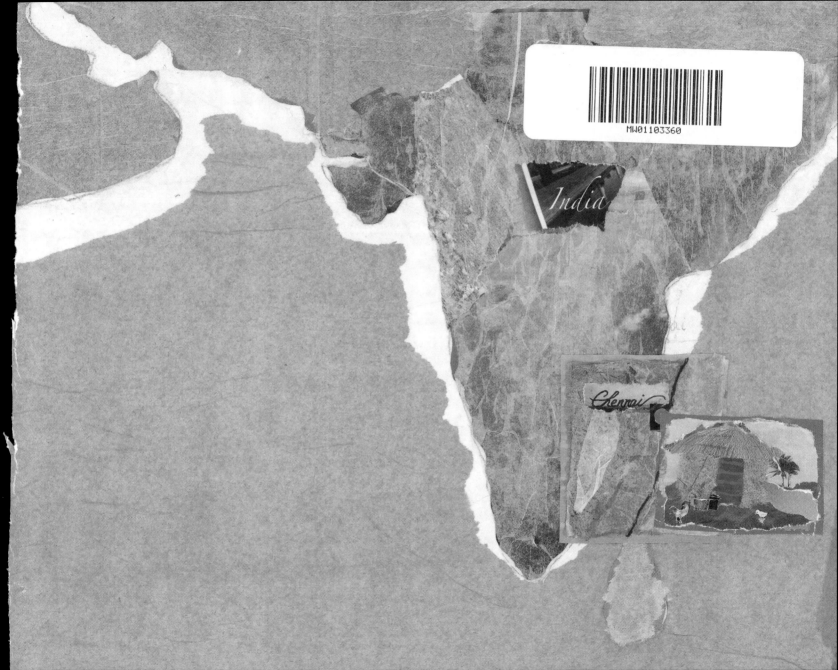

India

Chennai

Wings for a Flower is based on a true story.

Father
(Appa)

Mother
(Amma)

Kumudavalli
(Lotus Blossom)

Wings
for a Flower

Written and illustrated by Ellen Gaffney

three
bean press

Acknowledgments

Special thanks to Lotus and her family for their kind assistance and their openness in telling their story, and to Don Schoendorfer ("Dr. Don") at FWM for taking on the job of providing "wings" for our brothers and sisters who should not have to crawl on the ground. Thanks to Laurie for being my intrepid travel partner in India, and to Dr. CV Vadavana of Truth Ministries International, who works tirelessly to educate and elevate the poor, the disadvantaged and the disabled throughout the country of India. Thanks to Dr. Colleen Redit and her entire staff at Christian Missions Charitable Trust (Chennai), especially Sundari and Moses (RIP), who let us walk and work with them in the slum neighborhoods of Chennai and whose translations greatly enhanced my understanding of this special story. Thanks to family, friends, colleagues and teachers, who encouraged and taught me in this effort. Special thanks to my husband, whose unwavering support enabled the research and effort necessary to create the book; and to our three children, whose appreciation of and interest in the book provided an incentive to persist over the years. Not least, special thanks to my parents, who modeled love and respect and care for all, especially for children.

Wings for a Flower
Published by:
Three Bean Press, LLC
P.O. Box 301711
Jamaica Plain, MA 02130
info@threebeanpress.com • www.threebeanpress.com

Publishers Cataloging-in-Publication Data
Gaffney, Ellen
Wings for a Flower / by Ellen Gaffney.
p. cm.
Summary: A young girl in India loses the use of her legs. When doctors bring her a wheelchair, it changes her life dramatically for an outcome nobody could predict.

ISBN 978-0-9882212-6-0.
[1. Children—Fiction. 2. Physically Disabled—Fiction. 3. Wheelchairs—Fiction. 4. Free Wheelchair Mission—Fiction. 5. India—Fiction.] I. Gaffney, Ellen, Ill. II. Title.
LCCN 2013950872

Printed in the USA by Lifetouch through Four Colour Print Group, Louisville, Kentucky, in November 2013.

10 9 8 7 6 5 4 3 2 1

Ellen and Lotus, March 2005

About the Author and Artist

Wings for a Flower is Ellen Gaffney's first picture book. She learned about Lotus Blossom in 2004 and wanted to create a version of her story for children. Ellen soon realized she'd need to meet Lotus to be able to tell the story well, so, in March 2005, she went to Chennai to spend time with her. She came home with a firsthand account of Lotus' story and many reference photos and sketches. The trip to India made the people and places vividly real. It also made it clear that a simple chair with wheels can have life-changing results for a disabled person and his or her loved ones.

Ellen lives in the Boston area with her husband and their "released" service dog who happily works for food.

In the country of India, in the city of Chennai, in a hut by a river, a baby girl was born.

Her parents named her "Kumudavalli," which means "Lotus Blossom."

"A beautiful, healthy girl! Skin as soft as flower petals! Eyes like stars in the night sky!" her aunties exclaimed.

Appa watched proudly. Her uncles smiled and nodded.

In the mornings, Amma's
bangles called Lotus from sleep.

Amma hummed softly and
made tea.

Soon the patterns of Amma's
sari filled Lotus' fists as she
first stood, then walked.

Steamy hot days
s t r e t c h e d
slowly into steamy hot
nights. Rains began.

The burst of the monsoon
was followed by cooler,
drier days until the heat
began again.

In time, Lotus' sisters and
brothers were born, filling their hut
like rice cooked in a too-small pot.

Each day Amma said, "Come. We are
going for water now."

Picking up the baby, Lotus asked,
"When may I carry the water, Amma?"

As the oldest, Lotus taught her sisters
and brothers to help. "Appa can use that
wood," she'd say, and, "Pick up that bag
for Amma."

On hot, hot days, smells of cardamom
and cow patties, jasmine and diesel
hung in the air like clouds.

Horns honked.

Goats and chickens, cats and dogs
moved s l o w l y in the heavy heat.

Lotus cooled her hands and feet in the still, green river.

One day Lotus was too hot and too tired.

She could not get up.

Amma held a cool, damp corner of her sari on Lotus' forehead.

When Lotus woke from a sweltering dream, her clothes and hair were wet.

Amma said, "The fever has broken. You will grow strong again."

Days became weeks, but still Lotus could not walk.

Amma said, "We must see the doctor."

On the long trip, Lotus Blossom was not heavy in Appa's arms.

At the clinic, the doctor asked Lotus to stand.

She tried, but her legs were like empty banana skins.

The doctor told Amma, "Give her this medicine every day, two times per day. Come back in one year."

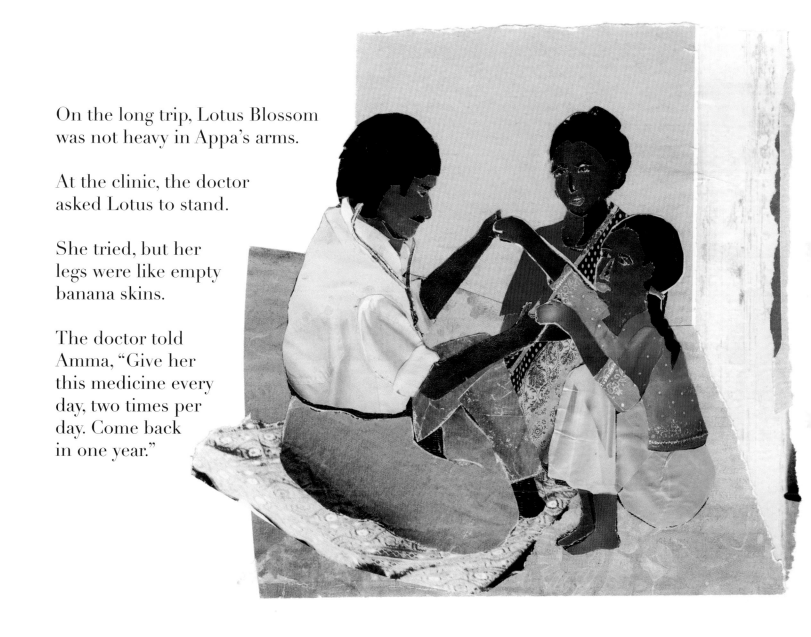

Back in their hut, baby brother played close to Lotus. Sister fed her. Amma gave her the medicine. But Lotus did not get better. She felt like a baby.

One year passed, and when the air was cool and clear, they returned to the clinic.

This time the doctor said, "She will not get better. She will be this way as long as she lives. It is a hopeless case."

The trip back to their hut seemed v e r y , v e r y long.

Lotus could not go to school. She could not play outside. Her legs would not carry her.

Inside the hut, she pulled herself slowly across the floor.

Many days and months later,
Sundari Aunty and Moses Uncle
came to their hut.

Aunty told Appa about the visitors
she had asked to come.

She said, "They are called Dr. Don
and Dr. Mike. They are bringing
something that might help Lotus."

Amma dressed Lotus in her best
clothes. Sister put sweet-smelling
jasmine in her hair.

Looking up, Lotus saw the tall
men in the doorway.

Dr. Mike had to bend
nearly in half to come into
the hut. He sat on the floor
and smiled.

He said, "Hi, Lotus. Can you
follow my finger with your eyes?"
and, "Now I'm going to check
your feet."

After a reassuring wink at Lotus,
he told Aunty, "She'll be fine in
the chair."

Then Aunty said to Lotus, "The
doctors have a gift for you."

Dr. Don was pushing a white chair
into the hut. It had wheels!

He said, "I made this in my garage.
Will you try it?"

Lotus looked down at her feet,
then nodded.

Dr. Don and Dr. Mike lifted Lotus
Blossom into the wheelchair.

"Just put your hands here and
push…."

They did not need to say more.

Lotus pushed the wheels once,
then again and again.

Brother called, "Come, Sister.
Come this way." He ran, shouting,
"Move! Move! Let her by."

He tossed the stones out of
the way, and Lotus was moving
outside by herself.

Her heart was so full she felt she
would be lifted out of the chair.

It was a chair with wheels,
but it felt like wings to her!

When the visitors left and night fell, Lotus closed her eyes and
slept with the peace of answered prayers.

The next day, Brother helped Lotus into the chair. She moved
all around the hut, then outside. She pushed on the wheels until
her arms trembled, then she rested.

Lotus' arms got stronger, and an idea came to her. Could she
work to make it come true?

Three years passed, and Sundari
Aunty came again with the visitors.

Amma helped Lotus through the
doorway and onto the path she had
ridden on so many times.

Three years ago, Lotus received a
gift she never expected.

Now she had a gift for Dr. Don—
something he could not expect.

This is what she dreamed about.

This is what she worked on.

She steadied her hands on the chair.
She put her feet on the ground.

Lotus took one step,
    then another
        and another
            and another.

Author's Note

I met Lotus Blossom and her family in March 2005 at their home in Chennai, India, where they generously shared their story. This book is a fictionalized account of Lotus' story. Her sudden illness, the hut, its neighborhood and the people in the story are depicted as I experienced them.

Lotus is but one of an estimated 100 million disabled people living in poverty around the world, without access to adaptive equipment other than that which can be made using cast-off materials. For these people, being physically disabled often means living in relative isolation, without acceptance, dignity or access to work or school.

In 2001, the Free Wheelchair Mission (FWM) was founded to respond to the hardship and isolation of the disabled poor. The organization produces large numbers of sturdy, inexpensive wheelchairs, which are given away with the help of local partner groups in developing countries.

Lotus Blossom received one of four prototype wheelchairs designed and hand made by Don Schoendorfer, founder of FWM. Don states that the joy on Lotus' face when she was lifted off the floor of her hut and into the chair drove him to pursue his vision of mobility for the poorest of the poor.

Lotus' astounding and unexpected restored ability to walk was beyond anyone's hopes. While most wheelchair recipients do not recover as Lotus Blossom did, they do have life-changing results: They are reconnected with their communities; their families and friends are freed from carrying them; and their basic human dignity is restored.

To date, hundreds of thousands of wheelchairs have been shipped to developing countries, assembled by local volunteers and given away, without discrimination, to people who need them.

www.freewheelchairmission.org

Note Regarding Lotus

Through the efforts of the Christian Missions Charitable Trust in Chennai, India, Lotus was diagnosed with acute onset rheumatoid arthritis. In 2006, with the financial assistance of a handful of American women, Lotus had hip replacement surgery and now has even greater mobility and reduced pain.

Africa